Published by Creative Education
123 South Broad Street, Mankato, Minnesota 56001
Creative Education is an imprint of The Creative Company

Art direction by Rita Marshall
Production design by Clean Tone Creative Consultants

Photographs by: AP/Wide World (Kevork Djansezian, Chris Gardner, Rusty Kennedy, Alex Trovati, Xinhua), Corbis (Bettmann, Neal Preston), Icon Sports Media (Tom Hauck, V.J. Lovero/SI, John McDonough/SI, Gerald Raube, Todd Warshaw, Wireimage.com), The Sporting News (Bob Leverone, Robert Seale), Sports Gallery Inc. (Brian Spurlock).

Copyright © 2004 Creative Education.
International copyrights reserved in all countries.
No part of this book may be reproduced in any form without written permission from the publisher.

Library of Congress Cataloging-in-Publication Data

Goodman, Michael E.
Kobe Bryant / by Michael E. Goodman.
p. cm. — (Ovations)
Summary: Introduces the life and accomplishments of basketball guard Kobe Bryant, whose high scoring game helped bring the Los Angeles Lakers three straight world championships.
ISBN 1-58341-248-4

1. Bryant, Kobe, 1978- —Juvenile literature. 2. Basketball players—United States—Biography—Juvenile literature. [1. Bryant, Kobe, 1978- 2. Basketball players. 3. African Americans—Biography.]
I. Title. II. Series.

GV884.B794 G66   2003
796.323'092—dc21
[B]   2002035148

First Edition

2 4 6 8 9 7 5 3 1

OVATIONS

KOBE

BRYANT

BY MICHAEL E. GOODMAN

Creative Education

REFLECTIONS

The Los Angeles Lakers were playing the Utah Jazz in the National Basketball Association (NBA) playoffs following the 1996–97 season. One more Jazz win and the Lakers would be eliminated. In the game's closing seconds, the teams were tied. Twice, Lakers coach Del Harris called plays to free 18-year-old rookie guard Kobe Bryant for shots to win the game. Each time, Kobe confidently put up the shot—and missed everything. Two air balls. LA ended up losing in overtime. The loss brought the Lakers' season to an end, and the team flew home that night.

Early the next morning, Kobe was in a high school gym near his LA home. He was practicing alone, working on the shot that had not fallen the night before. He was determined to make it the next time.

Determination and hard work characterize Kobe Bryant on and off the basketball court. He has always been mature beyond his years. His motto since childhood has been, "Know what you want to do, see what you want to do, and go get it." Early on, he set his goal at being a professional basketball player. Then he went after it.

The road to his goal has not always been smooth. He made a controversial decision to skip college and go right to the pros from high school, confident that he was ready to take on the best. He waited impatiently on the bench much of his first season, rose to sixth man his second, and became a starter in year three. He has never been hesitant in crunch time, and his confidence—combined with his skill and willingness to work hard—has helped him become a true All-Star.

Fueled by his desire to be the best in his sport, Kobe gives his all each time he steps onto the court, whether practicing alone or playing for the NBA championship.

EVOLUTION

When Kobe Bean Bryant was born on August 23, 1978, he received two important gifts from his father. The first was his unusual middle name: "Bean" was a shortened version of his father's nickname, "Jelly Bean." The second gift was an inborn desire to play professional basketball. Kobe's father, "Jelly Bean" Joe Bryant, spent eight seasons playing center and forward for NBA teams in Philadelphia, San Diego, and Houston, and another eight seasons starring for several different teams in Europe. Joe Bryant had size (6-foot-10 [208 cm] and 215 pounds [98 kg]), athletic skill, and a driving desire to compete. He passed these along to his son.

On Kobe's fifth birthday, his parents gave him another important gift, an official NBA basketball. That basketball quickly became the center

of Kobe's life. By the time he was six, Kobe could dribble and shoot the ball as well as kids years older than him. That year, Kobe and his family moved to Italy, where his father would be playing basketball.

Kobe and his two older sisters, Sharia and Shaya, had no trouble learning to speak Italian, and they loved living in Europe. Also, since their father's basketball schedule in Europe was not as hectic as it had been in the NBA, the family had more time to spend together.

Kobe's biggest problem was finding kids to play basketball instead of soccer. Kobe invented his own solo game, which he called "shadow basketball." He would imagine that shadows were other players on the court with him. He worked on moves to get around the shadow opponents for a layup or faked them out to give himself room to sink a jump shot.

While the Bryants were in Italy, Kobe's grandparents often sent them videotapes of American movies and NBA basketball games. Kobe was especially impressed with the skill and showmanship of Los Angeles Lakers All-Star point guard Earvin "Magic" Johnson. Magic had a special flair on the court and a constant smile as he played. He directed the Lakers' attack, which Los Angeles fans called "Showtime." Kobe wanted to be Magic

Two men in particular inspired young Kobe to pursue his dream of becoming a basketball star: his father, Joe Bryant, top, and the legendary Magic Johnson, bottom.

Johnson, and he wanted to be part of "Showtime." Soon he was incorporating Magic Johnson moves into his shadow basketball games. In those games, Kobe was the star of the Lakers.

Kobe and his sister Sharia joined a club basketball team in Italy that emphasized the fundamentals. Kobe learned the right way to move his feet on defense and to set his body for shots on offense. But Kobe was not content just to learn to play well. He wanted the excitement of competition.

"Kobe was always so serious about everything he did as far as sports. Always so intense," said Sharia. "When he was 8 and I was 11, we were in the same basketball league [in Italy]. The rest of the kids just wanted to play, and he was like, 'I want to win. There's 30 seconds left, and we're down by two; give me the ball.' I mean, he was into it. He's always been that way."

A lot of Kobe's competitive drive came from playing one-on-one games against his father. Jelly Bean never eased up on his son in those contests. Kobe had to fend off lots of flying elbows and body slams, but the competition helped to toughen him. He also learned how to be more alert

on defense and how to get off his shot against a much taller opponent.

When Kobe was 13, his father retired as a player and moved the family back to the United States. They settled in a Philadelphia suburb, and Kobe had to learn to think and talk like an American again. One of his biggest adjustments was relating to his African-American classmates, who had a slang and style he was not used to. He had to prove himself on the basketball court, too. On his first day of middle school, Kobe took on a challenge from one of the school's top players. He quickly won the game and gained the respect of his classmates.

Soon, Gregg Downer, the basketball coach at Lower Merion High School, heard about the middle school prodigy. "I watched him play for five minutes," Downer recalled, "and I said to my assistant coach, 'This kid's a pro. He's going to be a pro.'"

High School Hero

By the time Kobe entered Lower Merion High, the 14-year-old freshman was already 6-foot-4 (193 cm). He won a starting spot and led the team in scoring with an 18-point average. Despite Kobe's efforts, however, Lower Merion finished the season with a dismal 4–20 record. But the next year, both Kobe and the team showed remarkable improvement. Kobe upped his scoring average to more than 22 points per game, and Lower Merion made the division playoffs with a 16–6 record.

That summer, Kobe dedicated most of his time to playing basketball. He participated in six different leagues, sometimes playing more than 12 hours a day. He even began playing against college players in inner-city Philadelphia and practicing with some of the Philadelphia 76ers. "After a while, it began to pop into my head that I could play with these guys," Kobe recalled. "They respected me." He began to tell close friends about his new ambition—to enter the NBA right out of high school.

Kobe has won wide respect among fellow players and fans, as much for his generous, easy-going nature as his incredible quickness and high-flying style on the court.

"I'm going to be the one in a million who makes it," he said. "You see Magic [Johnson] and Michael [Jordan]? They made it. What's different about them from me?"

During the next two years, Kobe—who had now grown to 6-foot-6 (198 cm) and 220 pounds (100 kg)—led Lower Merion to the state tournament both seasons and to a state championship his senior year. Along the way, he broke the southeastern Pennsylvania high school scoring record once held by the legendary Wilt Chamberlain. During his senior season, Kobe averaged 31 points, 12 rebounds, 7 assists, 4 blocks, and 4 steals per game, and was selected as USA Today's National High School Player of the Year.

While basketball was the focus of Kobe's life in high school, he was not just a jock. He maintained a solid B average and scored more than 1000 on his SAT, a test that students who want to go to college must take. He also had a reputation as a good dancer and loved to show off his skill.

His classmates were especially impressed when Kobe came to his senior prom with singer/actor Brandy, whom he had met at a music awards show. Both teenage stars spent part of the evening signing autographs.

Then, on April 29, 1996, Kobe made an announcement to a crowd of friends and reporters gathered in the high school gym: "I've decided to skip college and take my talent to the NBA. . . . I know this is a big step, but I can do it. . . . I don't know if I can reach the stars or the moon. If I fall off a cliff, so be it."

Reaction to Kobe's decision was mixed. Many basketball scouts felt he should develop his skills in college before turning pro. Others thought that Kobe was ready, not just because of his game, but also because of his intelligence and maturity. They saw him as the NBA's next Michael Jordan. Kobe's family—always his biggest fans—supported his decision. His mother commented, "Kobe is a balanced young man. He's always stayed focused on what is really important. I don't worry with Kobe or any of my children because we have a great family foundation." Kobe's father added, "Hey, I would have liked Kobe to go to college for four years. . . . This was Kobe's dream. This is his life, so it was his decision."

Business and advertising executives quickly recognized Kobe's

Kobe leaped into the spotlight in 1996, at the age of 17, with his surprising announcement, middle, that he was turning pro right out of high school.

appeal to young people, and he was offered a multi-million-dollar sneaker advertising contract from Adidas, even before he was chosen in the NBA draft. Eighteen-year-old Kobe was already on his way to becoming a pro athlete and a millionaire.

Making waves with the Lakers

In the two months before the NBA draft, Kobe worked out for several NBA teams. He was particularly excited to perform for Jerry West, the NBA Hall-of-Famer who served as general manager of the Los Angeles Lakers. The Lakers had been Kobe's favorite team since his shadow basketball days in Italy. West was excited by what he saw in Kobe, too. "He was the most skilled player we ever worked out," commented West. Unfortunately, the Lakers had a late pick in the first round, and Kobe figured to have been selected long before LA's turn.

Kobe was a little disappointed when the Charlotte Hornets chose him as the 13th pick in the draft. However, his emotions quickly changed when he learned he had been traded to the Lakers in exchange for center Vlade Divac. Amazingly, Kobe was heading to Los Angeles. And the entire Bryant family, which had always done things together, packed up and headed to California with him.

Despite a rocky rookie campaign, Kobe soon found his niche within the Lakers, pairing with Shaquille O'Neal, opposite bottom, to return the team to glory.

Kobe didn't get off to a great start in Los Angeles. First, he broke a bone in his wrist during an outdoor pickup game and missed part of his first training camp. When he was finally able to practice, Kobe annoyed some of his teammates with his tendency to drive inside against bigger players rather than pass the ball. Instead of becoming part of "Showtime," he earned the nickname "Showboat."

The teammate most annoyed by Kobe's tactics was another newcomer to the Lakers, center Shaquille O'Neal, who had been signed as a free agent. Shaq considered himself the team's real star, and he didn't want to share the spotlight with a "green" teenager who wanted to hog the ball. Jerry West, however, was certain that the Shaq-and-Kobe combination would eventually click. The Lakers had not won an NBA title since 1988, but West believed his new duo would soon make LA champions once again.

Kobe had to work hard to earn playing time that first season, but that didn't dim his confidence or his determination. He focused especially on his passing and defense to make himself a better all-around player.

Kobe finally had his real "coming out party" during All-Star weekend in early February 1997. Playing in an exhibition game for NBA rookies, Kobe scored a record 31 points. The next night, he wowed everyone by winning the slam-dunk contest. In his final dunk of the competition, he made a spectacular between-the-legs move with the ball in midair and then stuffed it through the basket.

Back in LA after the All-Star weekend, Kobe got a chance to start several games and helped guide the Lakers to the playoffs. He played a small role in the Lakers' first-round win over the Portland Trailblazers, and got more playing time in the second round against the Utah Jazz. Then, Kobe suffered through his most embarrassing moment ever on the court, when his two last-minute air balls cost LA a chance to stay alive in the series.

Kobe became the Lakers' sixth man in his second season, and averaged more than 15 points per game, playing only half of most contests. Even though he wasn't a starter, Kobe impressed basketball fans around the country so much that they voted him to be an All-Star Game starter—the youngest NBA All-Star of all time. His number 8 jersey also became the hottest seller everywhere. Kobe had become a fan favorite and

In 1998, the 19-year-old player in the number 8 jersey turned heads in the sports world by becoming the youngest ever to play (and start) in an NBA All-Star Game.

was always surrounded by autograph seekers. Thrilled by the attention, Kobe never refused anyone an autograph or a warm smile.

The start of Kobe's third season saw the NBA, the Lakers, and Kobe himself involved in controversy. The year began late because of labor problems. Then, in the preseason, Shaq and Kobe began to snipe at each other, each vying to be recognized as the club's star. Many experts wondered if they would ever be able to play together effectively. The Lakers got off to a bad start, and coach Del Harris was fired. New coach Kurt Rambis promoted Kobe to the starting guard position. Kobe's average soared to nearly 20 points per game, and he earned a reputation as one of the league's top backcourt defenders.

In the playoffs, Kobe and Shaq really clicked for the first time. Kobe worked hard at getting the ball in to the big man, and Shaq's play inside freed up outside shots and driving opportunities for Kobe. "All those stories about me and Shaq, you can throw in the garbage," Kobe told reporters after the Lakers easily won their first-round series against Houston. "Look at us. We play great together." The improved "Kobe and Shaq attack" wasn't quite enough to get the Lakers by the San Antonio Spurs in the next round, but things were definitely changing for the better.

Off the court, Kobe found a new way to star also: he established the Kobe Bryant Foundation in 1998 to help young people at risk. The foundation raises money for several southern California charities that provide children with a safe place to play together or offer a shelter for children who are abused at home. Kobe and his parents continue to play important roles in the foundation, and Kobe spends a lot of his free time meeting with kids helped by the foundation.

Superstar status

When Phil Jackson, Michael Jordan's former coach with the Chicago Bulls, took over the Lakers for the 1999–2000 season, Kobe's career reached a major turning point. Jackson's triangle offense,

Kobe's phenomenal skill and unwavering confidence helped lift the Lakers to new heights at the turn of the millennium, earning Los Angeles a world championship.

which emphasized player movement and lots of passing, gave Kobe the opportunity to become a playmaker as well as a scorer. His improved offensive skills, combined with his intense defensive play, helped Kobe join the NBA's elite. That year Kobe was named to the All-NBA Second Team and the All-Defensive First Team. He also garnered something even more important, an NBA championship ring, as the Lakers wiped out the Indiana Pacers for their first title in more than a decade.

Kobe's amazing play at the end of overtime in game four of the championship series helped seal the Pacers' fate. The Lakers led the series two games to one, and the game 118–117, with only seconds remaining. LA guard Brian Shaw put up a shot that rolled off the rim. Suddenly, Kobe swooped in, grabbed the rebound, and put in a return to establish an unbeatable lead. "Kobe smelled victory at the end of the game and lifted us," said Coach Jackson. A few nights later, Kobe scored 26 points to spark the Lakers' title-clinching victory. At age 21, Kobe was a champion.

Kobe's personal life and business life also blossomed that year. He presented his 18-year-old girlfriend, Vanessa, with a magnificent six-carat diamond engagement ring, and they married in 2001. On the business front, Kobe earned lucrative endorsement contracts from sporting goods and soft-drink companies. He also purchased a half-interest in a basketball team in Milan, Italy, on which his father had once played. The former teenage sensation had truly become grown-up on and off the court.

Kobe earned two more rings following the 2000–01 and 2001–02 seasons, as well as two more berths in the NBA All-Star Game, and two selections to the All-NBA First Team. There was no doubt now that Kobe was among the best basketball players in the world.

While the debate continues as to whether Kobe Bryant will be as successful an NBA player as Michael Jordan, there is no doubt that he accomplished more than any other player ever before the age of 24. "It's going to be real scary when he's 24, 25, 26," his teammate Shaquille O'Neal once predicted. But Kobe Bryant has no fear about his ability to succeed. He plans to be thrilling fans—and scaring opponents—for many years to come.

Over the last few years, success for Kobe has come in the form of NBA rings and trophies, endorsement contracts, and the love of his wife, Vanessa, top.

VOICES

ON HIS FAMILY:

"From the enthusiasm aspect, his love to play, I am more like my father. But on the court, I'm more like my mother. She's like a pit bull. Her temper is like that! Very competitive. So I have the best of both worlds."
Kobe Bryant

"The backbone is the family. Once you have that, then everything else is cool. Whether you score 50 points or 0, your family is gonna be there."
Kobe Bryant

"I didn't beat my father one-on-one until I was 16. He was very physical with me. When I was 14 or 15, he started cheating. He'd elbow me in the mouth, rip my lip open. Then my mother would walk on the court, and the elbows would stop. He didn't do it to hurt me; he did it to make me tougher."

    Kobe Bryant

On his playing style:

"I love to pass the ball, but when it comes to crunch time, I click it on. There's no doubt I want the ball."

    Kobe Bryant

"Kobe has the ability to keep himself mentally in place, where even if he goes 3 for 12 one night, he believes maybe he can go 10 for 12 tonight. That's something you can't teach or coach. That's what makes him Kobe Bryant."

Derek Fisher, Lakers guard

"I have the ability to play other positions, but as far as categorizing me, I'm a guard. I was born a guard. I will forever be a guard. That's my game. I'm a scorer."

Kobe Bryant

"I really try to borrow things from every great player—Michael Jordan's post up, Reggie Miller's step back, little bits of every player. I'll take it and add it to my game."

Kobe Bryant

In 2002, Kobe scorched the nets with a career-high 56 points against the Memphis Grizzlies, helping him finish the 2001–02 season as the league's sixth-highest scorer.

On Comparisons to Michael Jordan:

"There will never be another Michael Jordan. I'm my own player. I want to be identified as my own player."
Kobe Bryant

"Let M.J. be M.J., and let the kid be the kid. M.J. paved the way for him, no question. But the kid's game has evolved into an all-around game. If he keeps putting on shows like he has lately, who knows how good he'll be."
Ron Harper, teammate of both Michael Jordan and Kobe Bryant

"Kobe's got Michael's skill and Michael's will. But Kobe came into the league when he was 18, and he's going to accomplish more."
Robert Horry, Lakers forward

"The kid is real good. I see a lot of myself in him."
Michael Jordan

Kobe's magnetism on and off the court has endeared him to fans around the world and earned him comparisons to the great Michael Jordan, top.

On his personal qualities:

"We view Kobe Bryant as one of a new generation of athletes who we think will transform sports in this country. Kobe is a kid with vision, a kid with a dream. I think his pursuit of that dream is going to be one of the most heartwarming stories in American sports over the next couple of years."

Steve Wynne, CEO of Adidas

"He's so good about it, I won't even go to the mall with him anymore because it's such a pain signing autographs. I've seen some of his teammates just turn down people in public, you know, but Kobe is always the one that says, 'Sure, no problem.' Eventually, it's going to be a negative, because he won't be able to do that without standing in the same place for four hours."

Sharia Bryant, Kobe's sister

"When Kobe came on the team, we said, 'What are we going to have to do extra for this kid? How are we going to watch over him?' But we haven't had to do anything. He's mature beyond his years."

Jerry West, former Lakers general manager

Thankful for his family's constant support, Kobe donates his time and money to help disadvantaged youth get a good education and realize their dreams.

ON HIS FUTURE:

"Kobe will be one of the best clutch players in NBA history."
Magic Johnson

"The funny thing is, when I first came into the league, everybody's expectations [for me] were down there, and mine were up here. Now everybody's expectations are up here, and mine are up even higher."
Kobe Bryant

"I want to be the best player who ever set foot on a basketball court."
Kobe Bryant

Near the end of the 2002–03 season, Kobe led the league in total points and field goals and hoped to spur his team to a fourth consecutive NBA championship.

OVATIONS